I0456294

BUMPS IN THE NIGHT
CREEPY CAMPFIRE TALES

Mark Leslie

STARK

PUBLISHING

BUMPS IN THE NIGHT: Creepy Campfire Tales
Copyright © 2019 by Mark Leslie Lefebvre

Originally published in 2012
Print edition published in 2019
Audiobook published in 2019

All rights reserved. No part of this publication may be reproduced, distributed or transmitted in any form or by any means, without prior written permission.

Stark Publishing
Waterloo, Ontario
www.starkpublishing.ca

The characters and events portrayed in this book are fictitious. Any similarity to real persons, living or dead is merely coincidental and not intended by the author.

Bumps in the Night / Mark Leslie Lefebvre
August 2019

DEDICATION

For J.P. Couvrette (1968 to 2012)

Thanks for so many good times, laughs, and the blessed memories of working together on those goofy high school skits, the school paper and ghost stories told around campfires when we were teens. I miss you, Couvy – so many of us do. But you should know that you still inspire me.

Table of Contents

INTRODUCTION

FOR ME, ONE of the best ways to hear a scary story is to listen to one being told around a campfire. There is nothing like the sense of community as a group of people huddle close to what is often the single source of light and safety, sharing eerie tales about those scary things that might exist beyond the safety of the firelight.

I have collected four tales here that might be ideal for such a setting, partially because they take place out-doors, but partially because a few of them were written specifically with oral storytelling in mind.

This collection was initially conceived and launched as an eBook to help showcase some of my fiction. Due to the demand of readers who wanted more or my work in print and audiobook, I have worked at expanding into those editions.

Erratic Cycles and *Almost* previously appeared in my story collection **One Hand Screaming,** and *The Shadow Men* appeared in the anthology **Northern Haunts** (edited by Tim Deal) In the original eBook version which was released in 2012 *The Pizza Man* was a previously unpublished story. In 2014 it appeared in a special limited-edition chapbook for Eeriecon 16 and then later, in *Night Cries: Nocturnal Screams, Volume 1* which came out in 2017.

I hope you enjoy these tales. And, if you're tempted to read one or more of them aloud at a campfire, go for it.

Mark Leslie
August 2019

ERRATIC CYCLES

CHARLES DEAN WEBSTER, attorney at law, sat very still in his '89 Toyota Tercel, frustrated over his predicament. Something — he had no idea what — had happened to his car. First there had been smoking and hissing and then the car had stopped running. That was the extent of his knowledge about what was wrong with his car. He was a lawyer, not a mechanic.

Dammit Jim, I'm a lawyer, not a mechanic.

He looked at his watch, taking his eyes off of the forest for only a very short time. It was a quarter past nine. As he lifted his head to look down the barren stretch of Highway 144, he caught the glare of the setting sun in his rearview mirror.

"Damn!"

He slammed a fist against the dash and then sat back once more and stared out the bug splattered windshield at the deserted highway.

Why me? he asked, and was quick to find an answer.

Why not you?

This was going to be your big case, your first major success, your big break. This was going to be the case that not only brought you a handsome sum but spread your name across the country. After winning this one, you were finally going to be someone.

So why not you? If you continue to believe such stupid glorified dreams, then why not you? Face the facts, schmuck: This is just another case.

And, being just another case, it had been nothing but a pain in the ass from day one. Getting stranded on a lonely highway somewhere between Sudbury and Timmins was just par for the course.

He looked at his watch again, but only a minute had passed since he'd last checked it. His eyes quickly returned to the wall of forest which ran never-ending along both sides of the highway. He couldn't shake the feeling that something was watching him from the forest.

No, not *something*, he corrected himself.

The Bush People.

He shuddered at that thought and considered turning on the radio to help alleviate his mood; but he was afraid that it would kill the battery. And he needed the battery in order for the hazard lights to keep working? Didn't he?

Dammit, it always came back to that, didn't it?

He hated the fact that he knew nothing much about how a car worked. But that had been his father's profession, not his.

When he was still young — very young — he'd watched his father closely. Anthony Webster would come home from the garage and spend as long as twenty minutes washing his hands and never really getting them clean. The tracks of his fingerprints were a permanent resting place for the grease and oil of his livelihood. Then, after supper, he would sit down in the living room with a beer in one hand and a remote in the other and grumble about inflation, taxes and the latest antics of the Toronto Maple Leafs. And the next day the cycle would repeat: *Work, a vain attempt to wash away the residue of that work, and when that failed, a cleansing of the soul with beer and bitching.*

Charles loved and respected his father who had never been anything but reliable and supportive. He'd always provided his only son with everything he could afford to give him and only once had he raised a hand to him — but in retrospect, Charles had deserved that quick slap after having verbally assaulted his mother in a typical teenager/mother argument. Anthony Webster was as close to the perfect father as any man could be.

But the last thing that Charles wanted was to be like him. He could never lead such a mundane existence. Charles wanted more than just money and a career. He wanted an exciting and fulfilling lifestyle. He didn't want his father's life of broken car after broken car — every day slaving over someone else's troubles and ultimately getting nowhere in life.

No, that wasn't for Charles. That wasn't what he wanted at all. He yearned to be a lawyer, to experience the lifestyle portrayed in the *L.A. Law* television series he'd loved so much; so he reached for it.

But he never got it.

Every case he took on held the promise of being *the* case which would move him up. But they never did. Instead, he slaved day after day over someone else's troubles, someone else's broken life, never moving up.

He ended up living the very lifestyle he had dreaded: His father's. Only, Charles lacked many of the things that his father had, including the knowledge of how a car worked.

Charles had been too engrossed in his own personal dreams to bother hanging around with his father and learning a few essential details about his trade.

And because of it, he was stranded.

Caught in the very trap he had attempted to avoid.

So it always did come down to that, didn't it? Running away from something only brought it down on you even worse.

His cellular phone was rendered useless by the remote location he was stranded in. He didn't even know how far it was to the next town, or at least to the next pay phone. If he knew, he might consider walking. It would be far better than sitting around waiting for another car to drive by.

Although it had only been fifteen minutes since he saw any traffic he was afraid that no one else would drive by. He'd never driven out of the concrete corridor before and had no idea of what to expect. Besides, even if someone stopped, would they even bother helping him if they knew who he was?

If only he could get to a phone and make one toll free call to the CAA.

Charles smirked and looked at his watch again without reading it. With his luck, his CAA membership would probably have run out, or for some stupid reason they didn't cover this area. Or perhaps the nearby CAA was run by one of the local groups that despised him. Wouldn't that be a cute confrontation? He wouldn't be surprised if any of these things happened — everything else had gone wrong so far.

It had started out as a simple case. His client, a Toronto-based company called Durban Lumber, had purchased a large chunk of land near Timmins for their logging operations. The only issue when Charles had picked up the case was a local band of Indians claiming traditional rights to the land. But Durban Lumber had purchased the land from the municipality and held legal ownership. It was a straightforward matter of Charles walking in, going through the motions, flashing the ownership papers, quoting a sample of similar past cases in which the defendant was triumphant, and hopefully settling it out of court.

Then a new development changed things. The native lawyers uncovered an old weathered copy of a document that the municipality had signed with the native leaders, recognizing the land as traditionally belonging to them. Because of a fire over two decades earlier at city hall, the municipality's copy of that document had been destroyed and forgotten.

And so the simple case had turned ugly. Durban Lumber was pressing the municipality from one side while the Indians were pressing them from another. The media had eaten the story up, of course, in the popular story of big business stepping all over the little guy.

The more sour the case turned, the more difficult it was for Charles to obtain the upper hand. The stress mounted, the tension increased and it began to get more than sour, more than ugly.

On his last visit to Timmins, a group of environmentalists and Indians greeted his plane at the airport with catcalls, rotten fruit and stones. Charles, the representative of the big bully, became the object of their hatred and anger. They all wanted a piece of him.

Things got so bad that instead of flying in to his next meeting in Timmins, Charles opted to drive. Not only would he arrive in an unexpected manner and hopefully undetected, but he could use the six or so hours that it would take him to get there to relax and sort things out.

It would be the first time he was alone in over seven years. Truly alone — without work and booze, his longtime companions.

After finishing a gruelling law school program, Charles had launched straight into his career. He started at the bottom, as most lawyers do, and had remained there ever since. He never once attributed his dire position to burn-out, but instead kept driving himself harder and harder, waiting for that one case.

At least in school when he botched a test or flunked a paper he had the chance of redeeming himself with another test or another paper before the final grades came out. But his career, he discovered, didn't work that way. Mistakes stayed on his record, without the possibility of being wiped out by future successes. There was no chance for redemption — there was only one thing. Plugging on.

So Charles had jumped from a life of study, work, party, sleep, to a life of work, research and more work. There were no study weeks or spring breaks where one could relax and then use the time to catch up on all the areas one had fallen behind in. There were no getaway weekends like there had been in school.

This was a career. This was life. This was not at all what Charles had expected or hoped for.

The only way he could cope was using a method he had learned by watching his father. He coped with the Webster method of bitching and booze. That soon became part of his daily ritual.

Years ago he had lived for the weekends and the promises that once school was finished he would be able to get on with living, with life, with being a free man in a free world. It wasn't long before he discovered that there was no such thing as freedom. There was no such thing as just living.

The barrage of clichés which his father spewed forth daily about the shit that life dealt an honest man were all coming true. Charles found himself not only repeating those same old tired clichés about life, but actually believing them.

Charles had discovered one night in the midst of an alcoholic haze that the cycle his life had taken was no better than his father's. Work like a bastard, then come home and drink like one. Only, his father also had a wife and a son. All that Charles had was work and booze.

It had become time to re-examine his life.

That was why this drive, this pilgrimage to Timmins, was supposed to be just the thing that Charles needed. It would be his way of being alone, without the work, without the booze. Just Charles and his thoughts. Six hours to finally reflect on what his life meant to him other than in the terms of a drunken man's armchair philosophy.

There was only quiet thought and gentle reflection as his car left the sprawling fringes of the city, headed north on Highway 400.

And then, several hours later, the car — the very means of his pilgrimage — broke down.

And Charles was alone.

In the middle of nowhere.

This newest development brought to him the real reason he had never let himself be alone for all those years.

Being alone scared the bejesus out of him.

He was surrounded on all sides, it seemed, by the thick foliage of the Northern Ontario wilderness. Wilderness that grew darker as the sun crept down somewhere behind the distant hills.

Wilderness that threatened to take him back to when he was ten and camping with his parents at Algonquin Provincial Park.

Back to the last time he had really felt *alone*.

Back to the time when he had first learned of *The Bush People*.

"No," he whispered, and it all came back to him in a sudden rush, as if the nineteen years between today and that dreadful evening had never happened at all.

He was returned to that night — back inside the body of a ten year old who was alone and lost in the thick of the night in the middle of nowhere.

He re-experienced it all.

The cold chill of the night wind. The smell of the nearby lake which carried the faint scent of trout. The unending rhythm of the crickets, forever bleating their cries of passion for the night, their chant that there was much more to the darkness than could be seen.

And the knowledge, the dreadful, painful knowledge that his parents were still sleeping in the tent, completely unaware that he was no longer tucked in his sleeping bag, dozing peacefully and protect beside them.

Charles had awoken with a demand from his body that he visit the outhouse. He had slipped out of his sleeping bag and began a quick search for the flashlight. He considered waking his father and asking him where it was, but the urge to go — now — was too great. He unzipped the entrance to the tent and headed down the trail to where he remembered the outhouse to be.

Only, either his memory had failed him or he had missed it in the darkness, because after walking for quite a while, Charles still hadn't found it.

He turned back, the cramps getting worse, and decided that he would wake his father after all.

But he came to a fork in the trail that he hadn't noticed on his way out. He took the one to the right, hoping that it was the correct one. But that trail led to another fork.

That was when he knew that he must be heading in the wrong direction.

He had been tricked.

By *The Bush People*.

The Bush People. His father had conjured them up that very evening in a story told by the campfire. They were the bogeymen of the wilderness that hid behind every tree, beneath every stone. They were numberless, faceless and without mercy. Their sole purpose was to trick little boys by leading them down the wrong paths, deeper into the forest away from the safety of their parents.

He opened his mouth to scream.

But he stopped himself with a sudden thought.

What if *The Bush People* didn't know where he was yet? What if they located their prey by listening for their screams? If he cried out for the help of his parents, *The Bush People* might also hear him and get to him first.

There was no way that he would scream.

The only thing left was to run.

He turned and raced down the path. Branches reached out from the sides of the trail, thin and invisible in the dark gloom. Each time they snagged him, he almost let out a yell, thinking it was a bush person touching him. They whipped at his face as he ran past them and tried to head down the proper trail, the trail that led to the safety of his parents.

The haunting cry of a loon echoed through the forest. To Charles it was the cry of another lost child trying to find his way to safety. Too bad pal, Charles thought. That cry just gave you away. Now they know where you are.

As he was thinking this, he collided with a wall of canvass stretched tightly across the path. He bounced back, sprawling to the forest floor and finally released the scream of terror he had been holding within.

No! he thought. They must have heard me. Now *I'm* caught too.

But then he heard the familiar grunt of his father. A command which was half-snore came from the other side of the canvass wall — which Charles realized was the tent — telling him that it was all right, to get back to sleep. His father must have thought that Charles was still in the tent and had screamed out while having a nightmare.

He quickly ran around to the front of the tent and slipped in. Then he crawled back into his sleeping bag which was still warm from the body heat he had left in it. He nestled there, the bag curled tight about his neck in an effort to keep out the chill of the night air. He lay there unmoving, waiting for the light of day as the pain of his cramps continued to grow.

But he would not go outside again that evening. Not without his parents — not until daytime when *The Bush People* were probably asleep.

And throughout the night, as the loon calls continued, Charles decided that they were *not* calls for help by lost children, but instead cries of pain and horror. The last desperate cries of the poor souls who had already been caught by *The Bush People*.

To keep his mind off of his cramps, he started counting the number of victims they had claimed. He quickly lost count.

Nineteen years later, Charles sat in his car, feeling a sudden urge to urinate. He no longer believed in *The Bush People*, realizing that his father had told him that story out of a fairy tale mentality. The same way that *Little Red Riding Hood* was supposed to teach children not to talk to strangers, Anthony Webster's tale of *The Bush People* was supposed to teach Charles not to wander from his parents when camping.

No, he no longer believed in *The Bush People*. But his fears — of being alone, being lost, and being in the forest at night — remained.

As the need to urinate worsened, becoming a tight unbearable pain, he told himself that he was being sill. Slowly, he opened the car door and stepped out.

The light from the opened car door spilled out onto the highway, pale and yellow. It mixed with the flashing red of his hazard lights. He looked at the light on the frail cracked pavement and then past it to the dark silhouettes of the trees against the grey night sky. He looked up, straight up to see more stars than he could ever see over the city. He saw in them the freedom of open space that this trip had originally promised him.

Freedom that was being threatened by the encroaching shadows of the trees which were far closer to touching the sky than he would ever be.

He hated them for mocking him so.

Unzipping his fly, he urinated in the middle of the highway.

Take that, he thought as his urine pattered on the dry dusty pavement. Piss on you, you stupid barren highway.

As he relieved himself, he kept his eyes on the forest. Black faced, it stared back at him. It was like a two-way mirror. He could sense, with every fiber of his being, that something was there, just on the other side of that blank face, watching him. But no matter how long he stared he couldn't see it. He could only see the trees.

Then, as he finished and zipped up his fly, he caught the glint of steel in the red reflection of the hazard lights. It stuck up from a patch of tall grass across the highway on the far side of the ditch.

Could it be a fallen highway sign?

He took a few steps across the highway and from there could see that indeed it was. Jesus, a highway sign. Maybe it would tell him exactly how far he was from Timmins, or perhaps from the next town. And if it wasn't too far, he could begin his hike.

It was much better than waiting for nobody to drive by all night and reliving ghost stories of his childhood.

His hope renewed, Charles took a few more steps. As he did this he felt a warmth and realized that for the first time in years he was in control of himself, of his fears. As mundane as trekking across a highway to read a fallen sign was, it meant to Charles that he was confronting his situation in an optimistic manner that took his destiny into his own hands. He had had it with merely reacting and avoiding. This time he was initiating a new chain of events.

He stepped off the solid pavement and onto the soft shoulder of the highway. The ditch was shallow, only about two feet lower than the highway, and Charles went through it easily and was on the other side, stepping through the tall grass toward the fallen sign.

Looking down at it, he wondered if instead of telling him anything important it would just be another SOFT SHOULDERS sign. He'd seen enough of them on Highway 144. He took a breath and bent over it.

As he reached down he thought he could feel a boney finger poking at his right shoulder.

Startled, he whipped his head around and saw that it was only a branch from a nearby tree which was sticking out over him. He relaxed again and took hold of the sign once more.

He couldn't read the sign in the dim light and so lifted it, tilting it towards the light emanating from his car.

He felt the boney poking again, this time closer to his neck. Then again. Then something had a hold of his shirt. He whirled around, dropped the sign on his foot, screamed in pain and stumbled forward, twisting his ankle on some unseen stone.

He fell to the ground, hard. The bleating pulses of pain shot up through his ankle to his ears, keeping perfect time with the red flashes of the hazard lights of his car. Another boney finger grabbed at his left shoulder and something pulled on his tie, chocking him.

Quickly, more boney limbs grabbed onto his body and pulled him slowly away from the highway. He struggled, trying to break free, but the chocking tug on his tie made him weak, useless.

In the dim red beat of the hazard lights he detected subtle movements above him which looked like tree branches bobbing to some soundless disco beat — but there was no wind.

He realized that the boney fingers were actually branches from the trees, and that they were passing him along to each other, deeper and deeper into the forest.

As he was being moved, dragged along the forest floor, his head collided with stones and stumps and he wondered vaguely, through the haze of pain and confusion, whether or not he would still be alive when the trees delivered him to *The Bush People*.

Then a new thought occurred to him.

Perhaps there were no Bush People. Perhaps there would be no destination, no end to this mad journey. Perhaps he would continue to be dragged along by the trees, helplessly stuck in yet another cycle until death finally claimed him.

"Please, God! Let the Bush People be real! Let them exist. Please . . ."

ALMOST

THE DARK WOODS were far from still. A strong wind made the tops of the trees bow. A low howl accompanied the wind as it forced its way around the branches and through the leaves. Orange and yellow corpses fluttered from the trees to the ground, never to be buried, merely trampled upon.

Muffled by the call of the wind, Dale Garrison crunched upon the newly fallen leaves as he ran through the forest. He stumbled to a tree and leaned against it, listening, watching.

Out of breath, he looked back over his shoulder. He'd gotten this far without them picking up his trail. But he couldn't rest long. The dogs would soon pick up his scent and they'd be on his tail again.

The horrid cost of freedom these days, Dale thought, running his left hand across his sweaty brow. He couldn't run like this all night. He'd have to find a ride or something, get out of his Sunnyside Institution uniform and flee the state before word of his escape got out.

It had been twenty minutes since he'd been free. No doubt the local stations had broadcast his escape by now. He had to be very careful. He was an easily identifiable suspect.

The wind howled louder, and he thought that he could pick out the sounds of barking in the distance.

Still out of breath, Dale stumbled forward and broke into a lurching run. A sharp pain stabbed through his side and he tried to ignore it. The tempting smell of freedom, like a carrot held before a starving horse, guided him onward.

Just when he thought he could bear the pain no longer, Dale staggered to a clearing. And before him he found exactly what he needed.

A pale grey Chevrolet was parked in the clearing on a hill overlooking a spectacular view of the town below. Dale could detect two figures inside the car through the steamy windows.

He slowly approached the car, crouching and trying to keep his breathing quiet. He hadn't yet figured out how he would overpower the people inside, as tired as he was, but he knew that he didn't have much time.

Nearing the driver's door, he remained low and peered in through the window. A glance at them would tell him if they would be much of a threat to his freedom.

Things hadn't changed much, Dale thought as he regarded a couple of teenagers making out. The male, thin and short, had his face pressed up against a blond haired female's face. Her hands danced up and down his back to the sound of a pop song on the radio. The male's hands deftly worked at unbuttoning the female's blouse.

The car had been idling. Dale could see the keys in the ignition.

Conflicting thoughts ran through Dale's mind. He wanted to continue watching. The sudden excitement of adolescent sex brought him memories of his own youth. It had been almost a decade since he saw real live breasts. But he needed to get the teens out of the car so that he could escape.

As Dale watched, feeling a stirring in his groin, he calculated his next move. Just as the boy had the girl's blouse open and cupped her breasts between his hands, the muffled voice of the radio announcer interrupted the song.

Dale moved to the back of the car, his plan already formed. All that he had to do was open the passenger door, pull the girl from the car and threaten to kill her if the boy didn't get out. He could then slip into the car and speed away.

From the woods came the distinct sound of barking.

They were getting closer.

Dale moved quickly around the back of the car, and in his haste tripped over something. He landed on his left hand and it twisted beneath him. He let out a yelp.

From within the car, the girl screamed.

Shit, Dale thought, cradling his left arm to his chest. The barking dogs were louder as they echoed in through the trees. As Dale slid forward on his left side, he could hear the boy and girl arguing within the car.

By the time he reached the passenger door, the arguing seemed to be over. As Dale reached forward and grasped the door handle with his right hand, the car started moving.

Searing pain shot through Dale's right arm as the car peeled away. He cradled the bloody stump at the end of his right arm to his chest and watched the car peel away down the dirt road, heading back to town.

Goddamn cheap doctors at the institution, Dale thought, listening as the barking dogs neared the edge of the clearing. They had the technology to provide him with a workable plastic right hand after the accident at the prison shop. But he was a criminal.

He moaned as he lay on the ground, the exhaust and dust from the car settling on his face. The dogs burst through the trees, the excited shouts of the cops not far behind.

They had the technology, but wouldn't waste it – or the money, for that matter – on a criminal slated for death row. Goddamn cheap doctors.

He almost had gotten away. He would have been able to open the door in time, if not for that useless prosthetic hand. As the first dog reached him, he vaguely wondered when they would discover the hook stuck in the door handle.

THE PIZZA MAN

CARL WAS HOVERING on the edge of consciousness when he became aware of the faint smell of pepperoni, tomato sauce and cheese. It was just strong enough to make him realize how long it had been since he'd had a filling meal.

And though physically exhausted – having spent the day moving into the old two-story brownstone just a few blocks away from the university – the scent of the pizza kept luring him by the stomach and slowly pulling him out of his sleep.

Carl's first conscious thought was of a jealous annoying nature. Sure, he was grateful that his cousin Rick, now in his second year of university, had allowed him to move into the newly rented four-bedroom home with two of his classmates, the very lovely Nancy and Marty. But Carl was a freshman, completely new to town and living "on his own" and still felt a bit like an outsider among the small group of four.

The thought that Rick and the girls had ordered a late-night pizza without waking and inviting him to join them just added to that sense of being an outsider.

There was a rustling outside his bedroom door and he sat up in the bed, now fully awake. The smell of pizza seemed stronger and although he couldn't see the door of his room as it opened he could hear the slight whispered sigh as it moved.

Because there didn't seem to be any lights on in the rest of the house – not even a sliver of light coming from down the stairs – a shiver spread through Carl and he felt an immediate surge of goose bumps swelling on his arms.

He instinctively reached for where the bed lamp had been back in his bedroom in his parents' home; but finding no light to turn on, no sense of familiar security to grasp, released a quiet whimper.

Through the darkness he heard a muted whispering from just inside his doorway and he gripped the sheets in fear. His eyes had become more accustomed to the dimly lit room and he could start to make out a figure standing in the doorway. A short figure.

"Carl?" It was a female voice. His panic quickly subsided as he recognized the voice and stature. It was Marty, the tiny girl with the long dark curly hair and big green eyes. Though he couldn't see her in the dark, his mind harkened back to how he'd spent much of that day when they were all moving furniture into the house gazing longingly at Marty's smooth, sun-browned legs and how her breasts strained against the confines of her t-shirt with the efforts of lifting and unpacking boxes.

And now here she was in his room. More goose bumps filled his arms, but for a different reason. Here was this beautiful, sexy girl, now in his bedroom in the middle of the night.

"Yeah?"

"Do you smell that pizza?" She found the light switch and turned it on.

Carl covered his eyes, squinting at her through his hands. "Uh-huh. Are Rick and Nancy cooking downstairs?"

"No," she said. "There's no light coming from down there. And besides, we don't have the ingredients to make a pizza."

There was a soft knock at the front door which carried clearly up the stairs and into Carl's room.

"What time is it?" Carl asked.

"Quarter to one,"

They waited in silence, staring at each other. There was another soft knock.

"Is someone gonna get that?" Rick yelled sleepily from his bedroom. "And while you're at it, keep it down, you two."

Carl hopped out of bed and his face flushed – he'd momentarily forgotten he was wearing only his underwear. He quickly grabbed his house coat from where it sat piled at the foot of his bed.

He headed down the stairs with Marty close behind him. They crept down in the dark and when they reached the bottom, headed down the hall toward the front door. As they got closer, Carl felt along the wall for the switch to the outside light and flicked it on.

The front porch light came on to reveal a dark figure backlit in the door window, a pizza box held high in his left hand.

The knock sounded once more, this time urgently.

The smell of tomato sauce and pepperoni was stronger than before as Carl stepped closer to the door. The figure was easier to make out now. Carl could see it was a male; a blond teenager with a few thick red pimples and a striking solid cleft chin. And even though he shouldn't have been able to see through the glass and into the darkened hall, his blue eyes seemed to follow Carl and Marty as they moved closer to the door.

"Pizza?" Carl asked through the closed door.

"Large pepperoni and mushroom,"

Carl opened the door. The smell of pizza was even stronger and more tantalizing. Carl heard his stomach rumble in response. He wanted this pizza, mistake or not.

"What's the damage?"

"Thirteen fifty," the blond teenager flashed a white toothy grin at Marty.

"I'll be right back," Carl said, turning to sprint up the stairs to get his wallet. When he got upstairs he found his wallet still in the back pocket of the jeans he'd thrown into the pile of clothes at the foot of his bed. He was just pulling the wallet out when he heard Marty scream.

#   #   #

"Are you sure you weren't sleepwalking?" Rick asked, lying in his bed facing the wall. Carl, Marty and Nancy were all standing in his bedroom doorway.

"She couldn't have been," Carl said. "We told you: I was there too. I saw him. Besides, you heard the knock yourself."

"All right. All right." Rick rolled over to face them. "You go downstairs. There's a pizza guy at the door. No one ordered a pizza. So far, no big deal. Mistakes happen, right?

"So Carl goes to get some money. Marty feels a draft, so asks the pizza guy to step inside. She steps around to close the door and when she turns around she can't see him. He's not there."

Trembling, Marty looked at the floor. "He vanished. Just like that. Gone."

"Look," Rick said. "People can't just vanish into thin air. It's impossible."

"Then what happened, Rick?" Carl placed a reassuring hand on Marty's shoulder. "When I heard Marty's scream I ran back downstairs and found Marty passed out in the hallway. The door was open and the pizza guy was gone."

Nancy nodded vigorously. Upon hearing Marty's scream, she had bounded out of bed, followed Carl downstairs and helped him revive Marty.

"Listen to yourselves," Rick said. "All the evidence is there that he *didn't* vanish. Here's what probably happened, Marty. When you turned around and couldn't see him he was probably standing in your blind spot. And then you freaked out, screamed and fainted." He paused to smirk. "And you scared the hell out of him. What would you do in his situation if some stranger asked you to step into their house at one in the morning and then turned around and screamed at you? You'd get the hell out of there, wouldn't you?"

"That does make sense," Nancy said. "Because the door was open. He must have been scared and ran off after Marty fainted."

They stood in Rick's room for a few minutes, reassuring themselves that everything was okay until Rick said that enough was enough, get out of his room so he could get back to sleep.

# # #

During the rest of the night Carl slept restlessly. He kept hearing a soft knocking at the door and was positive by the odor in the air that someone had brought a freshly cooked pizza into the house. A few times during the night, Marty called out from her room that she heard a noise downstairs. Just as many times Rick yelled out for her to shut up and get back to sleep.

# # #

When Carl opened the fridge to get himself and his three housemates a fresh round of beer, a partially torn and half-faded sticker caught his eye. Sure, he'd seen it yesterday, but suddenly something about the red graphic on it – the chubby man with a beard holding a steaming pizza – had a new familiarity to it.

He'd seen that same graphic on the pizza box the blond teenager had brought to the door the night before. The faded letters *Jimbo's Pizza* were still readable on the sticker as was the phone number.

It wasn't difficult convincing the rest of the house mates that ordering a pizza was a good idea, particularly since it had been four hours since they'd had supper: Their fine gourmet meal of hot dog wieners with a side of macaroni and cheese.

Inspired by the disappearing pizza guy from the night before, Carl suggested they order a large pepperoni and mushroom.

"It'll be here in half an hour or it's free," Carl said as he stood in the entranceway to the living room. "And it comes to fourteen twenty-five. C'mon, pony up the dough."

They all flipped their beer caps at him in response.

Carl couldn't help smiling. This was exactly how he'd imagined moving away and going to university would be; fun, freedom, playful adventure and -- his eyes settled momentarily on Marty, on the cute wrinkle in the corner of her eyes as she flipped another beer cap at him -- hanging out with gorgeous women.

Once they ran out of beer caps they started figuring out how to divide the cost of the pizza. It was easiest to round up, with tip, to sixteen dollars so they could each contribute four.

Carl had settled back down on a milk crate propped up beside the armchair Marty was sitting in and was about to ask about her home town, try to determine if there was a boyfriend back there, when there was a soft knock at the door.

Holding the money he collected, Carl got up and rounded the corner to the front door. The blond-haired teen from the night before smiled uneasily at him as the door opened. His blue eyes seemed a little more sunken and his face was quite paler than the previous night.

The pizza guy smiled at him. "Large pepperoni and mushroom. Thirteen fifty."

Carl took the pizza box and, having been ready with the sixteen dollars, turned and took a half step back to shoot a confused look at his room-mates. "It comes to thirteen fifty?"

"I thought you said it was fourteen twenty-five?" Rick asked.

Carl shrugged and turned back to the door.

The young blond was no longer standing in the doorway.

He stepped forward, peered out the door and was greeted by a soft September wind. The dark street was empty of both cars and pedestrians. He closed the door and went back into the living room with the pizza.

"Looks like this one is free," he said.

Hungry and drawn to the scent oozing from the box, they gathered on the floor around the pizza box. Rick tore cheesy pieces off and handed them around, nibbling on the strings of cheese from each one.

Marty shifted her piece from hand to hand. "Oh! Hot!"

Nancy sank her teeth in, starting to make the low satisfied moan of enjoying the taste. The moan quickly changed in pitch to a startled yelp and she threw the pizza slice into the air.

It landed face up on the carpet and the layer of cheese seemed to slide about on its own. A large beetle peered out from under the cheese and then scurried quickly beneath the sofa.

Marty dropped her slice and screamed as a cockroach hopped off her slice and scuttled down her arm. Rick quickly swatted it off and it hurried to join the beetle under the sofa.

"What the hell?" Carl mumbled, throwing his piece against the wall. It landed crust-up and a pair of bugs quickly ran from beneath it to hide under the armchair.

Rick dropped his slice into the box as they all jumped to their feet. The pizza still left untouched seemed to be slithering around in the box. The cheese moved as if the surface were a liquid on a tilting, rotating surface.

"Geeziz," Rick said, spitting out the bits of cheese he'd been chewing, and threw up. He stayed bent over, not quite finished and barfed again. Nancy joined him for the second round.

Rick, still green in the face, wiped his mouth and looked up at Carl, who was about to contribute the contents of his own stomach to the mess on the floor.

There was a loud knock on the door.

"Oh my god!" Marty yelled and leaned forward, retching.

Rick went to the door and Carl followed, pausing to flip the top of the pizza box closed.

The door opened and a dark haired middle aged man with an unsightly amount of pock-marks on his face stood holding an insulated pizza bag at waist level.

"Jimbo's pizza," he mumbled. "Large pepperoni and mushroom. That'll be fourteen twenty-five."

\# \# \#

The second pizza sat on the kitchen table uneaten.

Rick had taken a knife through it and discovered no roaches or bugs of any kind, dead or alive. Nonetheless, not a single one of them had any appetite. They simply stared at each other across the table.

"I don't understand it," Marty said, the green in her face almost completely gone.

"What does it mean?" Rick asked.

Carl got up and went down the hall to the living room. He came back with the bill that had been stapled to the first pizza box.

"What's that for?" Nancy asked, laying her head on Rick's shoulder. Rick stroked her short blonde hair.

"Take a close look," Carl said, "at the date penciled in. It says the fourth of September. But today is the third. And look at the year. It's last year's date."

Rick grabbed the bill from him and studied it. Then he looked at the bill on the pizza box on the table. "Today's date. Proper day, proper year."

"So we have three conflicting bits of information. The price, the day and the year. I'll bet if we called *Jimbo's* we might learn something more."

"Like what?" Rick asked.

"I'm not sure, but there has to be some explanation. Rick, why don't you call Jimbo's?"

"Why?"

"Well, we did receive a *defective* pizza from them."

Rick's eyes lit up and he got up from the table and picked up the phone. "You're right! They owe us." He dialed the number, told the person what happened and then described the delivery person.

"No," he said into the phone. "This isn't a joke."

His face went white and his mouth opened silently as he listened. He paused and then hung up the phone without saying another word.

"What?"

"According to the guy on the phone, this blond-haired kid disappeared in our neighborhood one year ago tomorrow. He's presumed dead, but his body has never been found."

# # #

Carl sat up in his bed, startled awake.

Was that a noise downstairs?

He carefully flipped away the covers and went to the door, flicking on his bedroom light.

A sudden blue flash lit the room as the switch clicked on, and then the room quickly receded back into darkness. He stood there, blinded and momentarily confused.

Of all the times for the bulb to die.

Grumbling, he stumbled in the dark over to his desk and lit the room with his small desk lamp, creating an eerie shadowy landscape of his bedroom.

Looking over at his digital clock, he saw it was 1:30 AM. He stuck his head out the bedroom door and confirmed that everyone else was sleeping by the fact that there was no light appearing at the cracks on the bottom of their doors.

He went back into his room, slipped back under the sheets and began reading the paperback sitting on his night stand.

Though his eyes passed over the words he wasn't actually reading them. Instead, his mind was going over the details he'd found when researching online about the teenage pizza boy's disappearance the previous year.

His name was Steve Buick. He was eighteen and had been working at Jimbo's Pizza for only 6 months when a call into this same neighborhood had been the last time he'd ever been seen. He simply disappeared, and his abandoned car was found in a nearby parking lot.

Carl had found four or five archived articles online from two of the local newspapers, but nothing after that. No indication of the teenager being found, either dead or alive.

He must have fallen asleep because the next thing he knew was being startled awake some time later upon hearing a noise – one he could only imagine as a bony elbow bumping against wooden paneling.

This time he left the bedroom and decided to head down the stairs, deciding not to wake anyone else up. He noticed a sliver of light appear under Marty's door as soon as he stepped on the stair second from the top and making a gritting moan of shifting wood.

So he wasn't the only one who had awakened.

He waited for her door to open and her head to appear and looked at her from the stairs with an *it's only me* smile. She smiled back sleepily.

"Did you hear that noise?" she asked.

He nodded. "I'm going to check it out."

"Why don't you wake up Rick?"

"No," he smiled. "Not after last night. He'll probably clobber me if I disturb his beauty rest. Tell you what; if I don't come back in two minutes, wake him and send him down."

He had said it jokingly, in the hopes it might relieve the tension, but Marty frowned disapprovingly at him.

"No," she whispered. "Don't go."

"It's okay," he forced a smile. "And stop that. You're scaring me."

He eased down the stairs and as he reached the bottom, the elbow hitting wood sound came again. He turned the corner to find the front door open and that the wind had blown it up against the wall, making that noise.

They must not have closed it properly in all the confusion over the two pizzas.

He walked up to the door and closed it. He had to push it extra hard before he heard the click of it latching closed. Yes, he thought. That was it. It simply wasn't closed properly.

He turned the deadbolt, ensuring it was locked, and made his way down the hall and back up the stairs. At the top, he explained to Marty that it had only been the door, and it was then they both seemed to realize he had been wearing only his blue briefs and nothing else.

Marty looked up from glancing at his jockey shorts to find him looking back, suddenly embarrassed, but trying desperately to pretend he wasn't.

As he rounded the top of the stairs, he noticed Marty was back-lit from the light in her room. He could make out her naked silhouette and the sides of the large satiny globes of her bosom. He shyly averted his eyes, feeling an instant stirring in his groin and shuffled past her into his room, hoping she hadn't noticed.

"Goodnight," he said, thinking that if this were a movie he would have simply continued to eye her naked silhouette and she would notice the growing bulge in his shorts and they would embrace, collapsing onto the floor in her room and make frenzied love, fade to black and roll the credits.

But this wasn't a movie; it was real. And he was too hesitant, too unsure, and probably too excited over nothing.

"Goodnight, Carl," She crossed from her door and headed to the bathroom. "And," she paused taking another glance down at the bulge in his shorts, "thanks for the . . . uh . . . unspoken compliment."

"Uh," was all he managed to mutter as the door to the bathroom closed. He stood there a moment, alone with his semi-erection and feeling even more stupid.

Still unsure what to do and not wanting to look like an idiot, he went back into his room, leaving his door open, and crawled under the sheets.

As his mind was racing with thoughts of Marty and whether or not she might come into his room, and what might happen between the two of them if she did, he heard the noise of the imagined elbow hitting the wall.

The door had blown open again.

But how?

He had definitely locked it.

Marty's voice came from the bathroom, calling him.

He yelled back for her to stay in the bathroom and keep the door locked. Not that a locked door seemed to help, but he didn't know what else to suggest.

Another noise came from downstairs. Another sound of something colliding into a wall. And this time it was louder, closer; coming from the bottom of the stairs.

Rick called out groggily from his room for them to stop making all that noise and get the hell back to sleep.

That was when Carl heard the creaking groan of the step that was second from the top. The sound pierced the dark night the way that fingernails on a blackboard cut through a silent classroom.

"Rick!" Carl screamed. "There's someone in the house!" But he knew *someone* wasn't the right word; he should have said *something*.

As Carl watched, a dark shadow moved across the hall toward his bedroom door.

And with it came the smell of tomato sauce, cheese and pepperoni.

The young blond teenaged pizza guy was standing in Carl's doorway. His cheeks were even more sunken and emancipated than before, almost melting off his face like so much mozzarella. The waxy lips moved slowly, revealing a few moldy black teeth.

Carl realized he was saying something.

"Pisssssssa," the tall thin figure slurred and as it went on to speak its top lip fell to the carpet. "Feffoni an mushoon."

It shifted another couple of steps into the room, reaching a thin, almost skeletal hand for Carl. As Carl watched, it continued to rapidly decompose in front of him.

Rick suddenly burst into the room with a wooden chair held over his head. He swung it down, breaking it across the intruder's back.

The blow sent the pizza guy forward onto Carl's bed, and he clambered along the bed, mouthing soundless words repeatedly. Carl bleakly wondered if its larynx had crumbled and fallen down its throat as he backed against the headboard of the bed.

Rick was lifting the chair again, looking at Carl, his eyes filled with questions. *What should I do?* His face seemed to be saying.

"He's already dead," Carl gasped. "You already tried once. We can't stop him like that."

A cold hand grasped Carl's bare foot, and Carl tried to thrash away from its cold moist touch.

What the hell was it trying to say?

"What?" Carl shrieked. "What the hell do you want from me?"

It pulled itself up Carl's legs and that was when Carl could see clearly into its eyes. He froze, and in the milky lens of its orbs he recognized something: fear.

It – no, not it; the teenager's name had been Steve -- Steve, was scared. Absolutely horrified. His eyes reminded Carl of something he'd seen in his own grandfather's eyes when he had been dying of cancer. It was a knowing, disturbed look that begged for the finality of death, the end of the pain.

"My God, Carl. It's all over you!" Rick yelled, and by that time Nancy and Marty were also at the bedroom door, standing behind Rick.

The creature, Steve, put a skeletal hand on Carl's shoulder and pulled himself up so that his face was level with Carl's. As his decayed lips moved, breaths of fetid air blew into Carl's face. The smell of rancid flesh churned his stomach.

But he could hear what Steve was trying to say.

"Th," Steve began. "Fh."

"Th. Fh."

Surf?

Nancy yelled out. "Do something, Rick!"

"Th. Tn. Fh."

"Like what? God, Carl. What can I do?"

"Th. Tn. Fh. Te."

Thirteen fifty? Thirteen fifty! Barely controlling the bile that rose in his throat, Carl asked: "Thirteen fifty?"

The flesh and bone head tilted and hope flooded through Steve's filmed eyes. For a brief second, Carl saw his own reflection in them. Steve's lips moved closer, quicker, more sure of the words.

"Thur. Tun. Fih. Tee." He repeatedly them frantically now.

"Rick! Get my wallet."

Rick fumbled with the junk on Carl's dresser, throwing a baseball cap off and discovering the black worn billfold beneath it. He grabbed it.

Carl stuck out his left hand and Rick placed the billfold in it. Steve repeated his relentless chant at a hurried pace, at times pressing his sour smelling facial flesh – what was left of it – against Carl's cheek.

Using one hand, Carl fingered open his wallet, found a bill and grasped it between two fingers, letting the wallet drop to the floor. He looked over at his hand. It was a green twenty-dollar bill.

"Thirteen fifty? Thirteen fifty?" Carl asked, screaming in a hysterical voice that cracked as he waved the bill in front of Steve's face. He let out a high-pitched cackle as he stuffed the bill into Steve's front shirt pocket. "Here you go. Keep the change!"

Steve's eyes remained on Carl and a smile that split his cheek open graced his face. He then stumbled off the bed and clambered out of the room.

They heard something bumping along the wall and tumbling down the stairs into the darkness below.

Moments later the front door slammed shut and the persistent scent of pizza was finally gone.

THE SHADOW MEN

I'LL NEVER FORGET the night that changed my life forever. It happened in the woods when I was ten years old.

It was dark; the air was crispy and chilly. Curious little sounds cut through the night – small animals rustling in the nearby bushes, the haunting call of a loon on the lake, leaves whispering in the breeze. And the air was charged with the smell of the still-burning embers of a recently doused campfire.

It was a night, in fact, not all that different than tonight.

I was sleeping in a four-man tent with my parents and younger brother and woke up with an overwhelming urge to pee. I crawled out of my sleeping bag, careful not to wake anyone else, slipped outside the tent and headed down the moonlit path to where I remembered the outhouse was.

Before I took more than a dozen steps I heard a noise behind me: the crack of a branch breaking underfoot.

With my hairs standing on edge, I manged not to let out a yelp as I turned.

There on the path not three steps behind me stood my little brother, a look on his cute button-nosed face like I'd just caught him sneaking a treat from the cookie jar.

"Jimmy," I whispered. "What are you doing?"

He stood with his right leg partially crossed over the left.

"Need to pee," he said, shifting his weight from foot to foot.

"Geez, Jimmy. If you had to go that bad, why'd you wait so long?"

"Because," he said, his six-year-old eyes wide and bright in the reflected moonlight, "the *Shadow Men* might get me."

I felt a shiver run down my spine despite the fact that I knew the *ShadowMen* were something my father had conjured up that evening around the camp fire. They were the bogeyman of the New Hampshire wilderness that hid behind trees and lurked in the shadows. Their sole purpose was to trick little boys down the wrong path in the woods, deeper and deeper into the forest and far from the safety of their parents.

Even at ten, I knew my father told the story to use for fun and perhaps partially to keep us from wandering far away from them; but when Jimmy said that I still felt a chill.

"The *Shadow Men* aren't real, Jimmy."

"Are too! Listen!"

At just that moment the haunting call of a loon echoed through the forest, delivering a deep shiver up the base of my spine.

"That's just a loon," I said, but the chill wouldn't go away.

"No. Listen, Charlie. It's a little boy. One that the *Shadow Men* tricked. He's warning us."

Frustrated with my brother – and, okay, a little frightened – I just wanted it to end; I didn't want to hear any more. So I thought I'd throw a good scare into him.

I turned and ran down the path. "Jimmy!" I called out. "Behind you! The *Shadow Men* are behind you!"

He let out a cry. "Wait!"

Able to see the path clearly in the moonlight, I ran fast, took a sharp turn and ducked down behind a low bush. Jimmy ran past me, still calling ahead on the trail for me to stop, panic rising in his voice as he seemed to think I'd gotten really far ahead of him. I had to put my hands on my mouth to suppress a laugh. But I stayed silent that way, listening to the padding of his footfalls on the packed dirt path and his calls for me to wait for him receding into the darkness.

His last cry was drowned out by the shrill call of a loon in the distance.

And I never saw him again.

But I hear him all the time.

Now, every time I'm out in the wilderness, out camping, I can hear my little brother's voice. Somewhere, masked within the sad, mournful, unearthly half-laughing, half-wailing cry of a loon, I can hear my little brother warning me that the *Shadow Men* are near.

Just listen for it and tell me what *you* hear..

BUMPS IN THE WRITING

Notes from the Author

I HAVE ALWAYS enjoyed learning a little bit about the stories I'm reading, a bit about the origin of the tales. For that reason, I have taken to inserting author notes whenever the opportunity presents itself.

If you enjoy a "behind the scenes" look at the stories you just read, then you might like what is about to come. If you'd rather just leave it at that, thanks for checking this little collection out. Hopefully it left you with some wonderful campfire chills.

# # #

ERRATIC CYCLES

(First Published in *Parsec* magazine – Volume 3, No 2, Feb 1999)
(Reprinted in **One Hand Screaming**, Stark Publishing, 2004)

I figured that any collection of campfire stories should include a "highway" story – one in which a motorist is stranded on a deserted highway.

Interestingly enough, one of the first drafts of this tale was entitled "Compact Car" and was a hitchhiker tale. The car breaks down, Charles gets picked up by another car, which (as these type of campfire tales often go), is a "ghost car" driven by a ghost. Then he gets pulled away into the forest at the end. One issue is that the ghost car bit was a fun stereotypical event, but didn't add much to the tale.

In further drafts of the story, I discovered more about Charles, about his fear of isolation, and the manner by which he was continuing to run from life rather than face issues head on. Thus, the whole ending with the trees pulling him forward made for a more satisfying terror, at least related to Charles' greatest fears.

# # #

ALMOST

(First Published in **One Hand Screaming**, Stark Publishing, 2004)

One of the most popular types of stories to tell around a campfire includes various versions of the "tale of the hook" – there are tame versions, and nasty blood-drenched ones.

One of the original versions of the tale sticks with the following structure: Two young lovers are enjoying an intimate moment in their car at a deserted spot when the radio broadcast is interrupted with an urgent public service announcement regarding an escaped convict on the loose; he is described as deadly and recognizable because he has a hook for a hand. People are told they should stay indoors call police if they see anything. The woman claims she heard a strange noise outside and wants to leave, the guy just wants to ignore it. They argue. Finally, realizing he isn't going to get lucky, he tears away in the car. And when he gets home to let the girl out at home and walks around to open her door for her (yes, this is an old tale back in the days of chivalry), he finds the hook stuck in the door handle. The fear comes from what had almost happened – if the boy hadn't pulled away at just that moment, the convict would have likely gotten into the car and killed them both.

Some of the bloodier versions of the tale have the boy going out to investigate a noise, telling the girl to stay inside the car. He never comes back. The girl sits in the car screaming because of an odd tapping on the car roof. In the morning, the police come, retrieve her from the car (this tale is before cell phones, of course), and try to keep her from seeing her beheaded boyfriend's head hanging from a branch over the car, dripping blood down onto the car.

Of course, there are hundreds of variations of this story, some gory, some a bit more eerie.

I decided to go with the classic version and try to see it from the point of view of the criminal.

That made writing the story a lot of fun.

# # #

THE PIZZA MAN

(First published in the 2012 eBook release of this book)
(First published in print in **Eeriecon Chapbook #14**, May 2014)

The very first version of this story was written late one evening in 1988 while I was in first year university and me and my house-mates were perturbed by two unsolicited pizza deliveries on the same night.

It was either a strange mistake (since we had just moved in the previous week), or a practical joke of sorts – but the part of my mind that finds dark and more disturbing ways to explain situations came up with the murdered teenager concept. So I went up to my room, turning on my Commodore 64 and started cranking out the story on my word processor. When I finished it several hours later, I printed it on my 12 pin dot matrix printer and read it to Maureen (who became Marty) and Nana (who became Nancy), two of my roommates, who quite enjoyed the tale; particularly the fact that it was set in our house and featured all of us. My cousin Rodney, who was the inspiration for Rick, shrugged it off, the same way Rick shrugged things off in the story.

It was a cute short tale, but there wasn't much to it other than a dead guy who kept showing up at the door and a bug-infested barfing gross-out scene.

So I kept picking away at the story over the years, working on turning the characters from caricatures and into developed people, (Modifying their names from our names and into the characters they would become) noodling with the plot, and coming up with the story.

I couldn't decide whether I'd call the story "The Pizza Man" in the hokey horror comic book style of story it was meant to be, or call it "Thirteen-Fifty" since paying the pizza guy what he was coming to collect is the key element that Carl uses to finally release poor Steve from his purgatorial existence.

Just prior to putting this collection together, I ended up sending this story out to a few beta readers to help me fix it up and determine the actual title – and that's how I landed on the title I used. I should point out that one of my beta readers, Bill Buick, bears absolutely NO relation to the dead pizza kid, Steve Buick, as I did compose that name half a dozen years before Bill and I ever met.

# # #

THE SHADOW MEN

(Previously published in **Northern Haunts:** *100 Terrifying New England Tales,* edited by Tim Deal, Shroud Publishing, 2008)

The Shadow Men was a result of digging back into the "Bush People" which I wrote about in *Erratic Cycles*. I quite enjoyed them and wanted to do a little something more with the concept. So when I saw the call for extremely short stories wanted for the **Northern Haunts** anthology, which was meant to be a fireside companion for scary stories set in the New England wilderness, I decided to write a story specifically for that purpose.

I quite enjoy micro-fiction and hope that this is a story that you as a reader might feel free to use yourself if you're ever asked to spin a quick campfire ghost story.

ABOUT THE AUTHOR

Mark Leslie is a writer, editor and bookseller who was born and grew up in Sudbury, Ontario, spent many years in Ottawa, Ontario and currently lives in Southern Ontario.

A bookselling veteran for more than twenty years, Mark has worked at virtually every type of bookstore, has sat on the Board of Directors for BookNet Canada and also been President of the Canadian Booksellers Association, was the Director of Self-Publishing and Author Relations at Kobo from 2011 to 2017 and is currently Director of Business Development for Draft2Digital. He has given talks across Canada and the United States, in London, Paris and Frankfurt on the bookselling, writing and publishing industry.

You can learn more about Mark and sign up for his newsletter at www.markleslie.ca.

Other Books by Mark Leslie

Canadian Werewolf

This Time Around (Prequel / Short Story)

A Canadian Werewolf in New York

Fear and Longing in Los Angeles (forthcoming)

The Desmond Files

Evasion

Coversion (forthcoming)

Sin Eater

Collateral Damage (Short Story)

I, Death

Short Story Collections

One Hand Screaming

Active Reader: And Other Cautionary Tales from the Book World

Snowman Shivers

Nocturnal Screams: Night Cries

Short Stories

A Murder of Scarecrows

Spirits

Anthologies (as Editor)

Campus Chills
Tesseracts Sixteen: Parnassus Unbound
Fiction River: Editor's Choice
Fiction River: Feel the Fear
Fiction River: Feel the Love
Fiction River: Superstitious

Non-Fiction / Paranormal / Ghost Stories
Haunted Hamilton
Spooky Sudbury
Tomes of Terror
Creepy Capital
Haunted Hospitals
Macabre Montreal

Watch for more at www.markleslie.ca.

www.ingramcontent.com/pod-product-compliance
Lightning Source LLC
Chambersburg PA
CBHW020649130626
46552CB00003B/1470